Cat & Mouse

A Delicious Tale

by Jiwon Oh

HARPERCOLLINSPUBLISHERS

For friendship

Library of Congress Cataloging-in-Publication Data
Oh, Jiwon.
  Cat & Mouse : a delicious tale / by Jiwon Oh.— 1st ed.
      p.   cm.
Summary: A cookbook makes Cat think about what a
delicious meal Mouse would make, but she dismisses the idea
because he is such a good friend.
  ISBN 0-06-050865-5 — ISBN 0-06-052744-7 (lib. bdg.)
  [1. Friendship—Fiction.   2. Cats—Fiction.
3. Mice—Fiction.]   I. Title: Cat and mouse.   II. Title.
  PZ7.O365 Cat   2003   [E]—dc21   2002007639

Typography by Elynn Cohen 1 2 3 4 5 6 7 8 9 10
❖ First Edition

To my family
and my friends

A long time ago,
a cat and a mouse
lived together.

They were best friends.

They washed their faces together.

They ate together.

They played together every day.

Cat loved to play dress up.

Mouse loved to paint.

One beautiful day,
they went fishing.

The hot sun made them sleepy,
so they took a nap.
Together, of course.

While they were sleeping,

Cat's old friend Monkey came to visit her.

He brought Cat a present.

Monkey gave Cat the world's best cookbook.

After reading the cookbook, Cat realized . . .

. . . that Mouse could be
the most delicious meal
in the world.

Now whenever Cat saw Mouse, she got hungry.
Cat could not stop thinking about Mouse.
He looked delicious.

Cat loved Mouse.
She knew she shouldn't eat him,
no matter how delicious he might be.
So Cat went far away.

Cat and Mouse had always been together.
They had never been apart.

Cat missed Mouse so much
that she couldn't eat or sleep.
This made her sick.

Mouse missed Cat so much
that he looked and looked for her.

And one day, he found her.